For Nara

Akinyi and her Mama, they set off in the gari.
Akinyi so excited, they were going on safari.

They drove past two tall twiga: a mother and
her child.
So many animals to visit as they drove out
into the wild.

They drove up into the hills, and back down
into the plains.
A baby elephant caught in the mud and
falling down again.

"STOP THE GARI, MAMA" Akinyi very
quickly said.
Then to the frightened Tembo, her Mama
she swiftly led.

"Our friend here is stuck, and we need to get her out!"

There was rope in the gari, but no other help about.

Akinyi comforted Tembo, held her close as they embraced.

"Mama will find us someone," and off Akinyi's Mama raced.

Tembo was scared and trembling, she was only just a child.

Too small to be alone, living out there in the wild.

Akinyi's Mama brought a Moran,
a warrior fierce and true.
"Give Tembo one end of the rope",
he said "We know just what to do"
"Moja, Mbili, Tatu." They counted **"One Two Three"**
A very **STRONG** pull and Tembo will be free.

Heave went the Moran, Tembo tried to push.
But they got nowhere, Tembo stuck fast in the mush.

The Moran went and got his friend, a goat herding Maasai.
They held the rope and pulled again, Tembo let out a big cry.
"Nne, Tano, Sita." They counted **"Four, Five, Six"**
We'll pull again and get Tembo out of this fix.

Tembo was very worried, but she tried to force a smile
You need a helping hand to survive out in the wild.

Tembo wasn't moving so Akinyi's Mama waded in.
Tembo was getting tired and starting to make a din.
The **NOISE** of an elephant is extremely very **LOUD.**
Even a solitary one, who is not talking in a crowd.

"Saba, Nane, Tisa" They counted **Seven, Eight, Nine.**
Tembo pushed her hardest holding fast onto the twine.

Nothing was changing, what were they going to do?

Tembo started to cry, she needed to go to the loo.

But there was no one else who could also pull and pull.

"Akinyi go and join", sang a nearby bird, a bulbul.

"But I am only little and like Tembo a small child."

"Everyone has gifts to share, even out here in the wild".

So Akinyi listened and they gave it one last try.

Akinyi asked her Mama "Should I really, can I?"

"KUMI" they shouted **"A BIG NUMBER TEN!"**

And if it doesn't work, then we'll try and pull again.

They all leaned back, Tembo gave a mighty push.
And out came Tembo, free to roam out in the bush.

"You see it was your strength, that helped Tembo to come free"
The bulbul songbird sang and giggled full of glee.

"Where is your Mama?" Akinyi asked Tembo.
Tembo was silent as if she didn't know.

Tembo started to cry, it was clear
she was alone.
In the great savannah plain, that
she called her home.

It can be a very lonely place, for a
little child.
Without Mama to care for you, out there
in the wild.

Akinyi hugged little Tembo, what else was there to do?
Standing there so small beneath the sky of blue.

Then they all went out to try reunite Tembo's mother
with her child.
Before they knew what badness had been out there in
the wild.

There had been some scary poachers, come
running at them with a gun
When Tembo had seen them she had run and
run and run.

Tembo was now a lonely orphan, yatima with no mum or dad.
She would have to live with Akinyi, as no other choice they had.

Tembo was not yet a grown-up adult, but did not feel like a child.
She was leaving all that she knew about a life out in the wild.

They drove past the manyatta village, said
goodbye to Maasai friends.
"KWAHERI" little Tembo shouted, the life she
knew now coming to an end.

Up through the farmer's planted wheat fields, on a
dirt road lined with grass.
It wound up and up and slowly, there was place for
Tembo's car to pass.

The new sights filled her with wonder, Akinyi soon
forgot her pity.
It was time for Tembo to start her new life in busy
Nairobi City.

They went through a small town and Tembo
waved her trunk to salimia.
She was feeling braver now and had a lot less
to fear.

Then they drove up and up past many trucks
with heavy loads.
Tembo and her new family to a life she didn't
know.

The road was hot and covered in many
stones that made it gritty.
It was the only one they could take to get
to big Nairobi City.

Then they got out at the viewpoint, the Great Rift
Valley down below.
When Tembo felt good and ready, then it would be
time to go.

Matatus, mikokoteni "Jambo, Jambo, fiti, fiti"
Noisy cars and many voices are the sounds of
the big City.

Akinyi, she loved playing with Tembo and her
stripy ball.
"IT'S TIME NOW FOR CHAKULA!" they could
hear her mother call.

"We'll need a lot of food" Akinyi's mother thought in her head.
To feed a baby elephant, and we don't even have a spare bed!

But Tembo ate most everything, and even liked Chapati
A favourite food of the girls and boys in Nairobi city.

Adventures make one tired, elephant or boy or girl.
They slept fast in Akinyi's room, Tembo's trunk in a
small curl.

And so they lived together, Tembo growing big
and pretty.
And it seemed she may have been suited to a
life in Nairobi City.

Tembo liked her painting, when Akinyi
taught her how.
She thought about her previous life, and
the one that she had now.

Tembo liked to learn new things, and so
that meant going to school.
She didn't want her new friends, to think
that elephants were fools.

She was growing BIG and STRONG and
broke her chair into itty-bitty.
It became clear she might be too big for a
life in Nairobi City.

She had to sleep outside, as she could not fit in Akinyi's home.
Eat din dins through the window, she needed much more space to roam.

Akinyi's Mama got a big truck to take Tembo
back home to the bush.
Promising that they would visit, Akinyi tried not
to cry or make a fuss.

Tembo was going back to where she would
not be such an oddity.
There's no life for a grown elephant in the
heart of Nairobi City.

The Kenya Wildlife Service helped Tembo's family to reunite.
Her aunties thought that they had lost Tembo on the day of that big fright.

Tembo taught them how to paint landscapes
with a brush on wet wet paper.
As she told them about the city matatus, noises
and skyscrapers.

Tembo was happy to be back where she had
lived as a small child.
We need to make it safe for elephants to
still live out there in the wild.

Kenya has more than 40 languages. The official language is English and the national language is Kiswahili. Kenya is also home to a new language called Sheng, a mixture of English and Kiswahili.

Many people in Kenya use more than one language when they speak. Kiswahili is spoken by millions of people all over the world. Our Glossary will help you to learn some useful words.

GLOSSARY

Gari   Car

Safari   Journey (now also an English word)

Twiga   Giraffe

Tembo   One of the Kiswahili words for elephant – the other is Ndovu

Moran   A Maasai man who has gone through a special initiation process (passed important tests)

Maasai – one of Kenya's tribes (a group of people with common cultures, customs

and language) a lot of whom still live traditionally and peacefully with animals.

BulBul   A Kenyan songbird that always has a lot to say

Poachers   People who illegally kill animals

Yatima   Orphan

Manyatta   Traditional Maasai homes

Kwaheri   Goodbye

Salimia   To greet (greetings are very important in Kenyan culture)

Matatu

Minivans that are used to transport people around the city

Mikokoteni

Hand carts used to transport goods around the city

Jambo

Hello in Kiswahili

Fiti

Sheng word for "I'm fine"

Chakula

Food

Chapati

Kenyan flatbread (originally from India)

Din din

Slang for dinner

HOW TO COUNT IN KISWAHILI

1 – moja | 2 – mbili | 3 – tatu | 4 – nne | 5 – tano
6 – sita | 7 – saba | 8 – nane | 9 – tisa | 10 – kumi

PRONUNCIATION GUIDE: KISWAILI IS PRONOUNCED JUST AS YOU READ IT HOWEVER THE VOWELS ARE:

A – ah
E – eh
I – ee
O– oh
U – uu

ABOUT THIS BOOK (AFTERWORD)

Akinyi's Mama wrote this book because she is worried that by the time Akinyi is grown up – there will be no elephants left in the wild. Everyone in the world has to work together to help stop elephant poaching.

Elephants are killed for their teeth. Their beautiful tusks are used as ivory to make decorations and jewelry. Both Akinyi and her mama think that ivory only looks beautiful on elephants.

In 1970 there were 167,000 elephants in Kenya. Now there are only 30,000.

Akinyi and her mama have a friend called Jim Justus Nyamu. Jim spends his time walking all over Kenya and the world teaching people about elephants and how we can learn to make the world, safe for them.

By buying this book, you are supporting Jim's work and helping to save elephants' lives. You can find out more about Jim and his work here: http://www.elephantneighborscenter.org/

If you find an orphaned elephant, do contact Kenya Wildlife Services http://www.kws.org/ who will help to look after them. Funny as it may seem, when they are little, elephants need special 24-hour care that you need to be trained to provide.

If you would like to foster a baby elephant, you can do so here: https://www.sheldrickwildlifetrust.org/

If you would like to find out more about Akinyi and her mama's adventures you can visit them at: www.creative-parenting.com

They would be happy to hear from you and even happier if you decided to visit Kenya and her beautiful elephants.